To my mum and dad
Alla mia mamma e al mio papà
F. C.

First published in the U.K. in 2008 by Gullane Children's Books, an imprint of Alligator Books Ltd,
Winchester House, 259-269 Old Marylebone Road, London NW1 5XJ, U.K.
First published in the United States of America by Holiday House, Inc. in 2008
Printed and Bound in China
www.holidayhouse.com
First American Edition
1 3 5 7 9 10 8 6 4 2

Library of Congress Cataloging-in-Publication Data
Chessa, Francesca.
Holly's red boots / by Francesca Chessa. — 1st ed.
p. cm.
Summary: Holly wants to play in the snow and needs her red boots,
so she and her cat Jasper search the house for anything red.
ISBN 978-0-8234-2158-9 (hardcover)
[1. Boots—Fiction. 2. Red—Fiction. 3. Cats—Fiction. 4. Snow—Fiction.] I. Title.
PZ7.C425224Hol 2008
[E]—dc22
2007035516

HoLLy's Red Boots

Francesca Chessa

HOLIDAY HOUSE / NEW YORK

Holly peered through her bedroom window. "It's snowing, Jasper!" she said to her little striped cat. "Let's make a great big snowman!"

"Can Jasper and I go and play outside?" Holly asked her mom.

"In your slippers?" Mom laughed.

"I promised my slippers I would show them the snow!" explained Holly.

"But your feet will get all wet! You need to wear your **red boots**."

Holly looked for her red boots.
"Aha! I see something
red under the table!"

The something red
was Holly's shiny . . .

red car.

"Now I won't get my feet wet!"
Holly said.

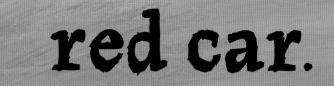

"Silly billy!" Mom chuckled.
"That won't keep your feet dry!"
Holly sighed. Where were her
red boots hiding?

Holly looked on top of the wardrobe. "Aha! I see something red here!"

The something red was . . .

a Mexican hat!

"It won't snow on my feet now," said Holly.
"You funny bunny!" Mom smiled. "A hat won't kee
your feet dry! You need those red boots!"

But Holly's mom
had a good idea,
and those red boots splashed
in puddles all day long!

the sun
was shining
and the snow had melted!
"It's all gone!" wailed Holly.
"Now my boots have
nowhere to go!"

TA-DA!

Holly and Jasper were ready. "Look, Jasper! I'm wearing my red boots. We can go out now!"

BUT . . .

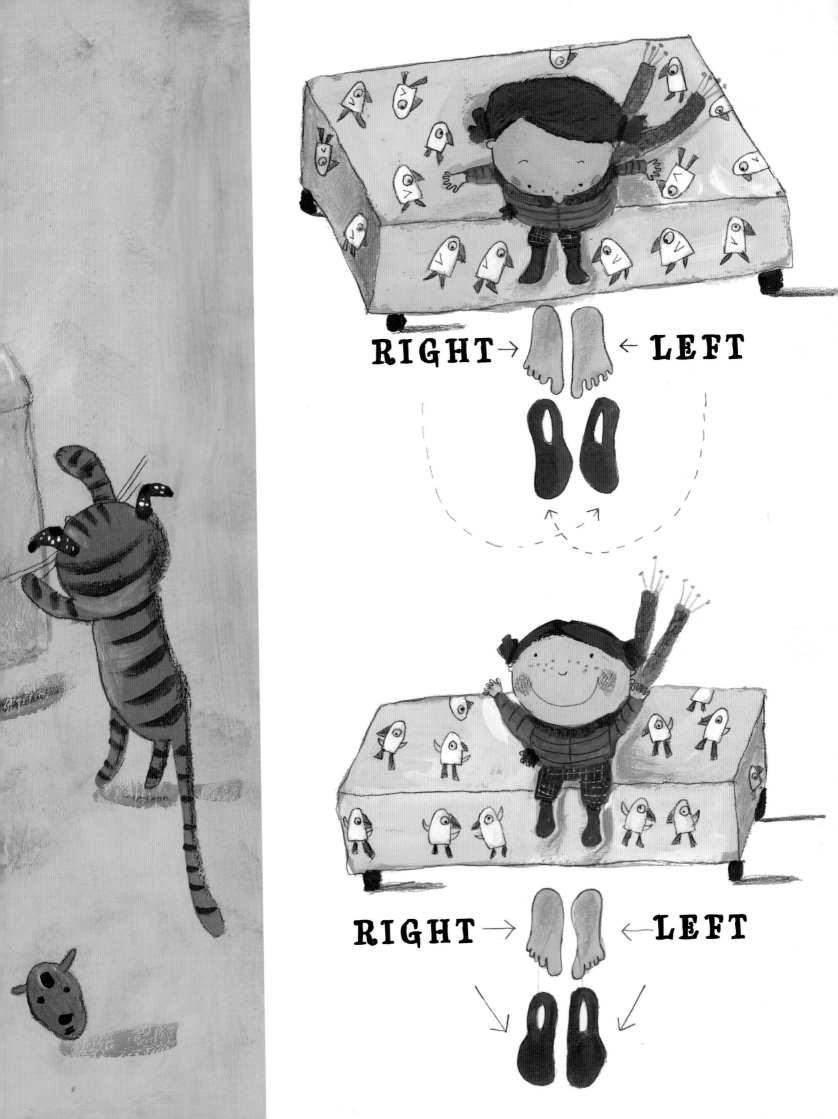

RIGHT → ← LEFT

RIGHT → ← LEFT

Holly tried to put on her boots,
but she put her right foot
in the left boot and
her left foot in the right boot . . .

until—at last—

Holly's red boots.
Holly's dinosaur had borrowed them!

There was only one more place to look—under the stairs.

And when Holly and Jasper opened the door, they spotted . . .

Holly found . . . a bathrobe, an umbrella, a bag,
a pair of gloves—and a pair of teeny tiny
red socks, just right for Jasper!

Jasper found something VERY interesting!

"Help me look, Jasper," said Holly.
"If we spot all the red things,
we might find my boots!"